28/10/2013

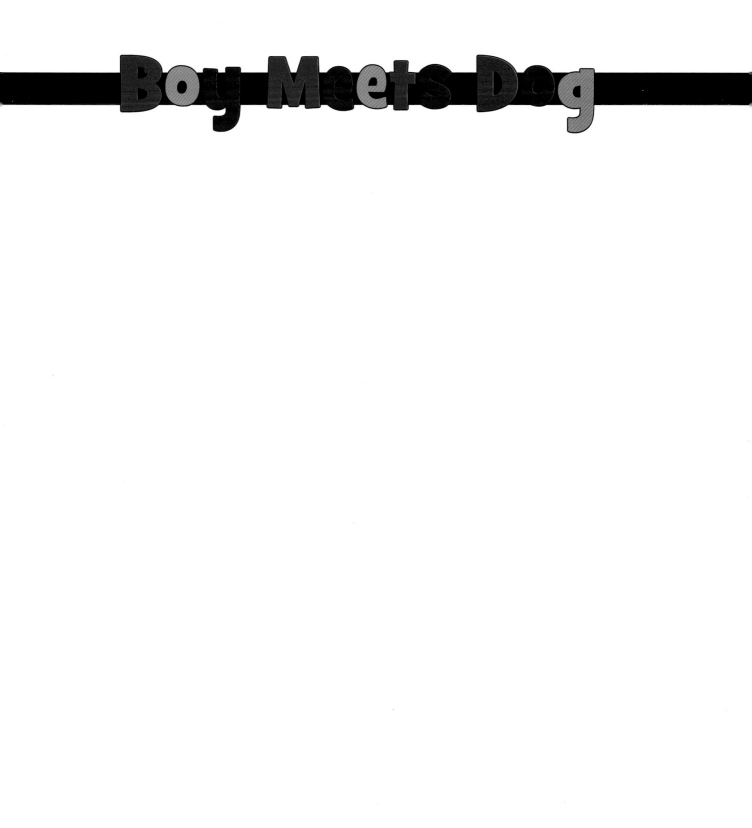

Boy Meets Dog

**For Seamus and Cassius Siddaway
and Damian and Sevrin Albert Cole — V.W.**

To my dog, Aiko — D.W.

Acknowledgments
Thank you to a puzzle-loving and quick-witted team of family and friends: Barbara Greeniaus, Fairlie Kinnecom, Steve LeGresley, Ian MacDonald, Mark MacDonald, Maryanne MacDonald, Lewis MacDonald and, most of all, Larry MacDonald. Also thanks to two great editors, Sheila Barry and Stacey Roderick, for their many good suggestions and to designer Julia Naimska and illustrator Dave Whamond for bringing boy and dog to life.

Text © 2013 Valerie Wyatt
Illustrations © 2013 Dave Whamond

Kids Can Press acknowledges the financial support of the Government of Ontario, through the Ontario Media Development Corporation's Ontario Book Initiative; the Ontario Arts Council; the Canada Council for the Arts; and the Government of Canada, through the CBF, for our publishing activity.

Published in Canada by
Kids Can Press Ltd.
25 Dockside Drive
Toronto, ON M5A 0B5

Published in the U.S. by
Kids Can Press Ltd.
2250 Military Road
Tonawanda, NY 14150

www.kidscanpress.com

The artwork in this book was rendered in ink and watercolor.
The text is set in GrilledCheese BTN.

Edited by Sheila Barry and Stacey Roderick
Designed by Marie Bartholomew and Julia Naimska

This book is smyth sewn casebound.
Manufactured in Shenzhen, China, in 3/2013 by C & C Offset

CM 13 0 9 8 7 6 5 4 3 2 1

Library and Archives Canada Cataloguing in Publication

Wyatt, Valerie
     Boy meets dog : a word game adventure / written by Valerie Wyatt ; illustrated by Dave Whamond.

ISBN 978-1-55453-824-9

     1. Vocabulary — Juvenile literature. 2. Word recognition — Juvenile literature. I. Whamond, Dave II. Title.

PE1449.W93 2013   j428.1   C2012-908358-5

Kids Can Press is a ᴵᴼʳᵁˢ™ Entertainment company

Boy Meets Dog

A Word Game Adventure

Written by Valerie Wyatt

Illustrated by Dave Whamond

Kids Can Press

Strange things happen if you change just one letter in a word.

A toy
could
become
a **boy**.

toy
boy

A **cat** could become a **dog**.

cat
cot
cog
dog

A **push** becomes a **pull.**

push
hush
husk
hulk
hull
pull

A **house** might become a **mouse**

and then a **moose.**

A **bus** can become a **car**.

bus
but
bat
bar
car

Tiny may become **huge.**

tiny
tine
line
lone
lore
lure
luge
huge

Black could become white.

black
slack
stack
stalk
stale
shale
whale
while
white

Heat can turn to cold.

heat
head
held
hold
cold

Rain can change to **snow.**

rain
raid
said
slid
slip
ship
shop
show
snow

As **light** becomes **night**,
a **broom** turns into a **spook**.

broom
brook
crook
crock
chock
shock
shook
spook

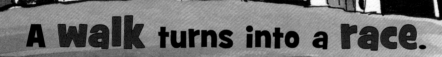

A **walk** turns into a **race**.

walk
talk
tack
rack
race

Safe becomes whew!

safe
sane
sand
send
seed
seen
teen
then
when
whew

Woof becomes whew!

woof
goof
goop
coop
chop
chow
chew
whew

whew!

A **boy** could become a **toy**.

But a **dog** is too loyal to change.

Lewis Carroll, author of *Alice's Adventures in Wonderland*, invented the game of word ladders, which he called Doublets, in 1877 as a Christmas gift for two girls. He gave the girls a pair of words, and they had to figure out how to get from one to the other by changing just one letter. A year later, he held a Doublets contest that ran for several months in a British magazine. The game has since "gone viral" and appears in many forms and places. It is most commonly called word ladders, word links or word chains.

Here are two word ladders Lewis Carroll came up with:

four	head
foul	heal
fool	teal
foot	tell
fort	tall
fore	tail
fire	
five	

And here are a couple to try yourself:

1. Turn calf into bull.
2. Turn fast into slow.

Solutions

2. fast, last, lost, loot, soot, slot, slow

1. calf, call, ball, bull

to change one word into the other. the best solutions are those that take the fewest steps There is no one right answer to a word ladder. But

Make your own word ladders

Think of two words of equal length and see if you can get all the words that link them. Some tips:

- Make sure your first and last words can be changed into other words. So, for example, you can turn broom into spook because both broom and spook have other words that they can be changed into. You can't change broom into ghost, though, because there is no word ghost can be turned into by changing just one letter.

- Don't just try the first word that pops into your head. For example, if you want to change great into another word, list all the words you can think of that can be made by changing just one letter (greet, treat, groat, etc.). If one doesn't work, maybe another one will.

A note to parents and teachers

Playing word ladders is a great way to

- improve vocabulary (keep a dictionary handy!)
- help learn spelling
- discover how some letter combinations often appear together in a word
- see the different uses of vowels and consonants in words
- have fun playing around with letters and words (try saying the word lists out loud — poetry!)

Word ladders are also no-fuss, no-mess and portable — all you need is a paper and pencil.